DATE DUE

E	#62398

PET   Petersen, P.J.
AUTHOR

Some days, other days
TITLE

DATE DUE	BORROWER'S NAME	ROOM NUMBER

SOME DAYS,
OTHER DAYS

SOME DAYS, OTHER DAYS

P. J. PETERSEN
Pictures by Diane de Groat

CHARLES SCRIBNER'S SONS   NEW YORK
Maxwell Macmillan Canada   Toronto
Maxwell Macmillan International
New York   Oxford   Singapore   Sydney

Charles Scribner's Sons Books for Young Readers
Macmillan Publishing Company
866 Third Avenue, New York, NY 10022

Maxwell Macmillan Canada, Inc.
1200 Eglinton Avenue East, Suite 200
Don Mills, Ontario M3C 3N1

Macmillan Publishing Company is part of the
Maxwell Communication Group of Companies.
First edition   10 9 8 7 6 5 4 3 2 1
Printed in Hong Kong on recycled paper

Library of Congress Cataloging-in-Publication Data
Petersen, P. J.
Some days, other days / P. J. Petersen. — 1st ed.   p.   cm.
Summary: Jimmy is reluctant to get out of bed, because some days
at home and at school are good days but some are bad days.
ISBN 0-684-19595-X
[1. Family life—Fiction.   2. Schools—Fiction.]   I. Title.
PZ7.P44197So 1994   [E]—dc20   93-3871

The illustrator wishes to thank Bryan Arsham and his parents, Marilyn and Ron,
for being such enthusiastic models. Appreciation also goes to Oreo and
Princess for their patience and occasional cooperation.

For my mother, Alice Lottie Winters Petersen

P. J. P.

"Good morning, Jimmy," Mom called.
"It's time to get up."

Jimmy sat up in bed. "I don't want to get up," he said to himself. "I don't know what kind of day it's going to be." It might be a good morning, but it might not be.

Some days they had waffles for breakfast. Waffles covered with strawberries. And there were enough strawberries so that he had berries in every bite. With some left over.

Other days they had cereal. And sometimes they were out of Jimmy's cereal, and nobody had remembered to get more. So Jimmy had to eat his dad's cereal, and it was plain and soggy and blah.

Some days his baby brother, Sam, laughed when Jimmy came into the kitchen. And he reached out his arms for a hug. And he smacked his lips and said, "Yum," while he ate his cereal.

Other days Sam wouldn't hug anybody. He cried and fussed and banged the tray of his high chair with his spoon. He dropped cereal on the floor, and Jimmy stepped in it.

Some days, when Jimmy's bus came, his friend Mark had saved him a seat. They sat right behind the driver and watched the cars go past. And they talked about horses and trucks.

Other days the bus was full, and Jimmy had to sit by a big kid. And the big kid never gave him enough room. So Jimmy ended up hanging off the edge of the seat. And the big kid didn't talk to him at all.

Some days, when he got to school, all the kids wanted him to play with them. "Over here, Jimmy." "Play with us." "Be on our team." "We saved you a swing."

Other days the teams had already been chosen, and the swings were all taken. And there weren't any extra balls. So he just had to stand around and wait for school to start.

Some days, when he painted a picture of his house, it looked just like his house. And he put a smiling sun in the sky and drew his whole family out on the lawn. And everybody said, "That's a great picture."

Other days the house looked as if it were falling down. And people thought it was an upside down ice-cream cone. And the red paint ran down his brush and onto his hand, and then he scratched his nose and got red paint all over his face.

Some days, at recess, he got to check out a basketball. And he and Mark ran out to the courts. And on Jimmy's first shot, the ball went right into the basket. And other kids said, "Way to go."

Other days there were no balls left. He had to join somebody else's game. And he had to wait a long time for a shot. And when it was his turn, he missed the basket by three feet, and the ball came back down and hit him on the head. And everybody laughed.

Some days, at lunch, there was good food in the cafeteria: macaroni and cheese, a fruit salad, and an oatmeal cookie. And all his friends sat at his table. And some of them didn't like oatmeal cookies and gave theirs to Jimmy.

Other days there was meatloaf with dark brown gravy. And no place for Jimmy to sit except with the little kids. Or the big kids. And the woman on duty told him to hurry up and sit down.

Some days, after school, there was a baseball game in his street. And he got to play. And when he came up to bat, he didn't strike out. He hit a high one over the pitcher's head.

Other days there was no ball game. Or there were just big kids playing. And they would only let him be an outfielder, so all he did was chase balls. And they wouldn't give him a turn at bat.

Some days Mom and Dad fixed dinner while Jimmy set the table. After they finished eating, they sat back in their chairs and talked about what they had done that day. And Sam smiled and laughed.

Other days Mom was late, and Dad cooked dinner. And he forgot and cooked the peas until they were too soft. And Sam cried and fussed and dumped his peas on the floor, and Jimmy stepped in them. And nobody talked after dinner.

Some days, after Sam was in bed, Dad or Mom would read Jimmy a story. Sometimes they would both sit with him. And all three of them would take turns reading.

Other days everybody was busy after dinner. And Sam would stand up in his bed and yell for a drink of water every five minutes. And then when Mom and Dad said, "No more water," Sam would cry and cry. And if Jimmy wanted a story, he had to read one by himself.

So Jimmy just sat there in bed. He thought maybe he would stay there all day.

Mom rushed in. "What's the matter, Jimmy?" she asked.

"I don't know what kind of day it's going to be," Jimmy said. "So I think I'll just stay in bed."

"It might be a very good one," Mom said. "And you wouldn't want to miss a minute of it."

"But it might be a horrible one," Jimmy said.

"Well," Mom said, "we'd better make it a good one. Let's start with a big hug. That way, the day can't be all bad." She gave Jimmy a hug and lifted him out of bed.

Jimmy kept his arms around her. "What are we having for breakfast?" he asked.

"Waffles," Mom said. "With strawberries."